Jesus Is for Me!

Chariot Books™
David C. Cook Publishing Co.

Christine Harder Tangvald
Illustrated by Donna Kae Nelson

Dedicated to my son, Leif Arne Tangvald
He is so good—for me
C.H.T.

For Cecilia Winger
Because the best things in life just happen
D.K.N.

Chariot Books is an imprint of David C. Cook Publishing Co.

David C. Cook Publishing Co., Elgin, Illinois 60120
David C. Cook Publishing Co., Weston, Ontario

JESUS IS FOR ME
©1989 by Christine Harder Tangvald for text
and Donna Kae Nelson for illustrations.

First Printing, 1989

Printed in the United States of America

93 92 91 90   5 4 3 2
ISBN 1-55513-740-7
LC 88-70664

Who do *you* think is the most important man there ever was in the **whole wide** 🌍 world?

Here are some clues:

1. He was born in a 🏠 stable.

2. One time, during a whirling, swirling ⛈ storm, this man walked on top of the 〰 water!

3. He is God's only Son.

4. He really likes 👨‍👩‍👧‍👦 children . . . like 👧👦 ME!

Who can he be?

I think the answer is _____.

Did you say **Jesus**? You did? Good for you!

You see, long long ago, in a 🏠 stable in Bethlehem, the most important person in the **whole wide** 🌍 **world** was born.

He was baby 🪺 Jesus.

His mother 👰 Mary wrapped baby Jesus in soft cloths and laid Him gently in a 🛖 manger, filled with fresh, sweet 🌾 straw.

👼 Angels told the 🧑‍🌾 shepherds to go and worship baby 🪺 Jesus.

I wish I could have seen baby 🪺 Jesus, too. He was born for 👧👦 ME!

Place
Angel
Sticker
Here

Baby Jesus was born for ME.

Luke 2:1-20

On that dark holy night, God hung a bright ⭐ star in the sky. God's ⭐ star shined down on baby 🍼 Jesus.

👳 Wise Men followed the bright, shining ⭐ star. They traveled a long way to **worship** baby 🍼 Jesus to bring Him wonderful 🎁 presents.

It was the most important birthday anybody ever had.

I'm glad baby 🍼 Jesus was born for 👧👦 ME!

Wise Men came to worship Jesus.

Matthew 2:1, 2, 9-11

Do you know what Jesus did when He grew up? He did lots of things that **surprised** and **amazed** people.

One time during a whirling, swirling ☁ storm, 🧔 Jesus walked right on top of the 〜 water. "How can You do that?" everyone asked. It was a **miracle**.

Another time 🧔 Jesus fed a huge crowd of hungry people with only five small loaves of 🍞 bread and two 🐟 fish. "How can You do that?" they asked. It was a **miracle**.

These stories about 🧔 Jesus are in the 📖 Bible for 👧👦 ME!

"How can you **do** that?"
It was a miracle!

Matthew 14:22-33; Luke 9:10-17

Sometimes Jesus is called the **Good Shepherd**. Do you know what a shepherd does?

A shepherd is someone who watches flocks of sheep.

A shepherd is gentle and kind, and he loves his sheep.

Jesus is gentle and kind.

Jesus cares for and loves me just like a shepherd cares for and loves his sheep.

I'm glad Jesus is my **Good Shepherd**.

Place
Hands
Sticker
Here

Jesus thinks I am **important**.

Luke 18:16, 17

Jesus has lots and lots of ♡ love. He never ever runs out. He has plenty of ♡ love for everybody.

And His ♡ love will never change—ever.

The 📖 Bible says

🧔 Jesus ♡ loved 👧👦 me yesterday.

🧔 Jesus ♡ loves 👧👦 me today, and

🧔 Jesus will ♡ love 👧👦 me tomorrow . . . and the next day, and the next day, forever and ever and ever!

Forever is a long, long time.

I'm glad 🧔 Jesus ♡ loves 👨‍👩‍👧‍👦 children like 👧👦 ME! I'm glad 🧔 Jesus will ♡ love 👧👦 me forever.

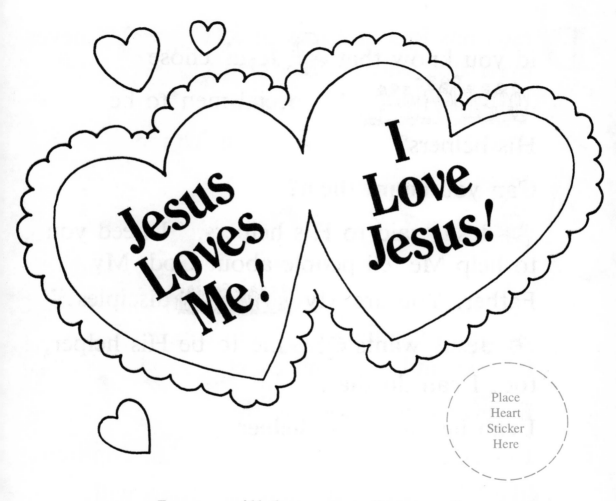

Jesus will love me **forever!**

Hebrews 13:8; I John 4:19

Did you know that Jesus chose

12 special men to be

His helpers?

Can you **count** them?

Jesus said to His helpers, "I need you to help Me tell people about God, My Father. You are My disciples."

Jesus wants me to be His helper, too. I can do that.

I can be Jesus' **helper**.

Jesus chose **Place 12 Sticker Here** special men
to be His **helpers**.

Matthew 10:1-4

Did you know that 🧔 Jesus is my very own **Savior**? He is!
He won a **victory** for 👧👧 ME!

Have you ever seen a ✝ cross like this one: ✝ ? The ✝ cross reminds me that 🧔 Jesus died for my sins.
Because of 🧔 Jesus, all my sins are **forgiven**.

And because I believe in 🧔 Jesus, do you know what will happen?
I will have life with Him forever!
First He will be right here with me on earth. Then I will be with Him in Heaven.

I **do** believe in 🧔 Jesus.
I really, really do.

Place
Cross
Sticker
Here

Jesus is my very own **Savior.**

John 3:16; 6:47; 11:26

But when 👤 Jesus died, He did not **stay** dead. No, He did not!

On the 1, 2, 3ʳᵈ day, an 👼 angel rolled the huge ◯ stone away from His tomb, and God raised 👤 Jesus from being dead. It was God's best miracle. His disciples were so ☺ happy.

Do you know what God did then? God took 👤 Jesus up up up into heaven. Now, 👤 Jesus watches over 👧👦 me all the time. And He sends His 🕊 Holy Spirit to live in my life.

I'm so ☺ happy that 👤 Jesus is my very own **Savior**.

Place
Flower
Sticker
Here

God **raised** Jesus from the dead
. . . for ME!

Matthew 28:2-7; Mark 16:6; Luke 24:50,51

H ere are some things I know:

1. I know that 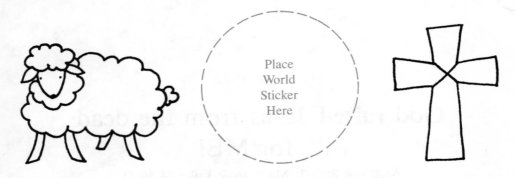 Jesus ♡ loves and cares for me. He is my **Good** Shepherd.

2. I know that Jesus thinks I am **important**.

3. I know that because I believe in Jesus, all my sins are **forgiven**, and someday I will go to heaven.

Place
World
Sticker
Here

4. I know that  Jesus wants me to be His **helper**.

5. I know that Jesus is my very own friend and **Savior**!

Yes, Jesus is the most important person there ever ever was in the **whole wide** world.

And I know Jesus is for ME!

Draw a picture of
yourself here.

I'm so glad that Jesus is for me!